Hi,
I am Lila
and this is my story

LILA
AND THE NEW BULLY

Ife Akanegbu

My Cute Prairie
www.mycutestories.com

To every child that ever ventured on this strait called life.
Thank you for reading my books

-Ife Akanegbu

Lila and the new Bully by Ife Akanegbu
Published by My Cute Prairie
Tumbler Ridge, BC

www.mycutestories.com

Illustrations by Parvez Alam.

ISBN: 978-1-7779621-1-1(Hardcover)   ISBN: 978-1-7779621-0-4(Paperback)
ISBN: 978-1-7779621-2-8(eBook)   ISBN: 978-1-7779621-3-5 (Audiobook)

First Edition: December 2022

The author wishes to acknowledge the insight and support of Tracy Krauss,
Chris Norbury, Nwora Okafor and family, Sanya Segun, and Joeline Akanegbu.

Lila looked around as she followed her mother into her new school. Everyone seemed very warm and friendly. She could be happy here.

Her mother's face was beaming. Lila knew that meant she was super happy. She smiled at her daughter, joy in her eyes.

"Baby, this is my dream school for you."

Lila followed her mother into the main office with a smile.

Principal Office

While they sat to meet with Mr. Dan, Lila couldn't help but wonder if her mother would tell her new principal why she was transferring out of Summerhill Elementary in the middle of the school year. She hoped not. The last thing she wanted was people to feel sorry for her for being bullied. She just wanted to forget it had ever happened.

After a quick meeting with the new principal, Lila was introduced to her new fifth grade teacher. Although the students had already left for the day, Miss Janet brought Lila to the classroom.

It was cozy, with beautiful paintings hanging on the walls. Lila knew she could be happy here.

The next morning, Lila was one of the first people in the classroom. She went to the desk Miss Janet had said was hers and took out her pencils. A few minutes later, a girl sat down beside her.

"Hi! I'm Laura. Are you new here?"

"Yes, I just changed from Summerhill Elementary."

"Oh, you're going to love it here. And I just know we're going to be great friends."

During their lunchtime, Lila studied the various paintings. The artwork belonged to the winners of the annual class art contest, the handiwork of students who had passed through the class over the past several years. Would her work ever end up on that wall?

Lila drew, but she didn't know whether her art would be as pretty as that.

"Get out of my way!"

Lila spun around to see who had shouted. A girl was barreling towards her. Lila darted out of her path and watched the girl walk to her seat in the corner of the room. Turning to see if anyone witnessed what just happened, she was embarrassed to realize that some of her classmates were looking at her.

Lila quickly went to her own desk, burying her head in a book so no one would see her cheeks turning red. Why had the girl yelled at her? What had she done wrong? And, why did no one say anything?

The lunch break ended and the class returned to their seats. Mama had told the teacher that Lila was a good student, so she did her best to pay attention to Miss Janet. However, even though math was one of her favorite subjects, Lila had trouble focusing on the lesson. She could not forget about the girl that had shouted at her.

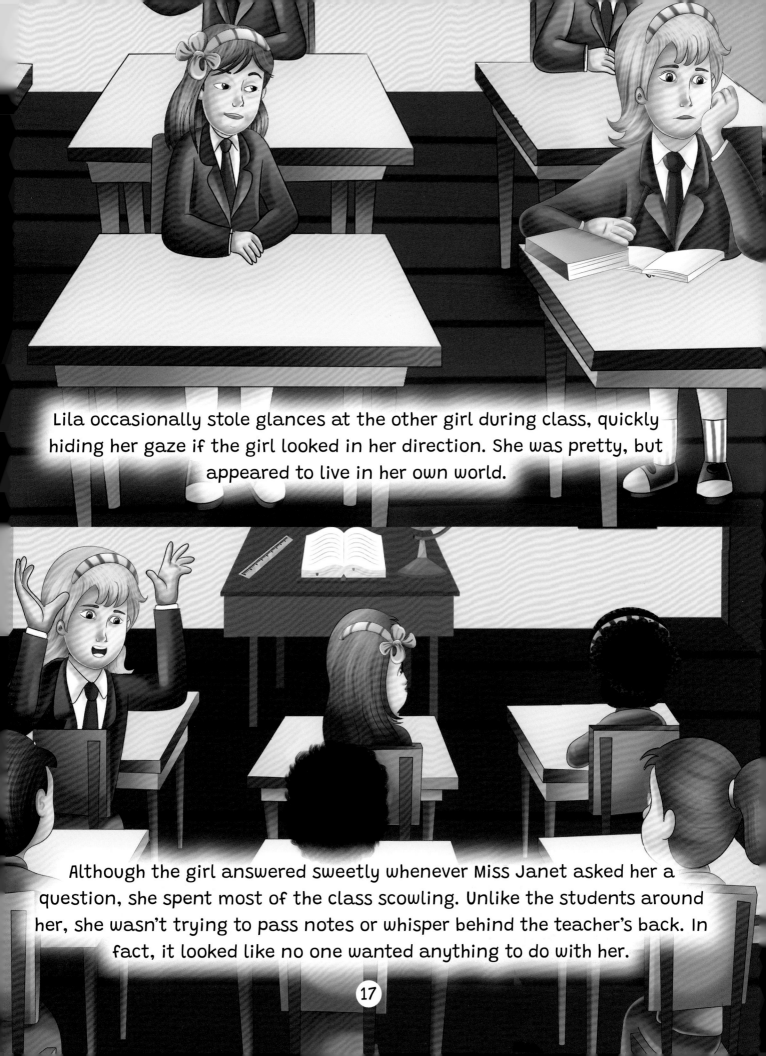

Lila occasionally stole glances at the other girl during class, quickly hiding her gaze if the girl looked in her direction. She was pretty, but appeared to live in her own world.

Although the girl answered sweetly whenever Miss Janet asked her a question, she spent most of the class scowling. Unlike the students around her, she wasn't trying to pass notes or whisper behind the teacher's back. In fact, it looked like no one wanted anything to do with her.

After school, Lila decided to ask Laura about the girl.

"Oh, her name's Kima. No one likes her."

Lila frowned. "Why not?"

"She's so mean. She's always yelling at everyone."

"She didn't seem so bad during class."

Laura shook her head. "She's okay with Miss Janet, although sometimes she gets in trouble for being rude. But, when the teacher isn't around, she's a monster."

"Doesn't she have any friends?"

Laura shrugged. "Maybe a few? I'm not sure."

"But, why is she so mean?"

"Who cares?"

Lila was surprised by her friend's attitude.

If she knew what made Kima mean, maybe she would be able to avoid her anger, she was trying to do the same back in her school before Mama moved her here.

Lying in her bed that night, Lila wondered why children became bullies. She had had these same thoughts for the past several months. Maybe it was because they didn't have any friends? She knew that Mama believed bullies were bad kids, but Lila wasn't so sure.

Her mind wandered to the bully in her former school. Kane was sociable enough, nobody would say that he had trouble making friends like Kima seemed to have, but he had always been so mean to Lila.

She had spent so many nights crying because of the things he said. She hadn't told her teacher. She was hoping she could figure out why Kane behaved the way he did so she could help him change. But one day, someone else told Mr. Clarke they had seen Kane being mean to Lila. As soon as Mama heard this, she pulled her out of Summerhill.

Lila let her mind wander back to Kima. Maybe this time she could do something. Kane had seemed a happy kid with many friends and good grades, but he enjoyed being mean to Lila. Kima on the other hand... well, the girl always sat alone and everybody ignored her. A sudden idea formed in her mind and Lila jumped off the bed to reach her backpack. She was determined to solve this.

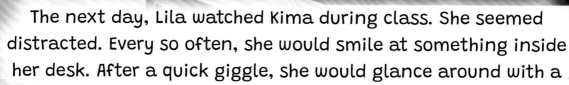

The next day, Lila watched Kima during class. She seemed distracted. Every so often, she would smile at something inside her desk. After a quick giggle, she would glance around with a scowl, as if suddenly remembering she was in class.

Nudging Lila with her elbow, Laura gestured to Kima with her eyes.

"I've never seen her smile. Wonder what she's looking at."

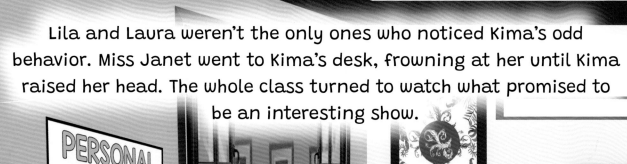

Lila and Laura weren't the only ones who noticed Kima's odd behavior. Miss Janet went to Kima's desk, frowning at her until Kima raised her head. The whole class turned to watch what promised to be an interesting show.

Miss Janet held out a hand. "Turn it in."

Kima glared at the teacher. "Turn what in?"

"Whatever it is that is more interesting than this history lesson."

Kima shrugged, pulling a piece of paper from her desk and holding it above her head. It was a picture of Miss Janet with a mop, labeled Miss Janetor.

As their teacher snatched the page from Kima's hand, most of the class laughed. But Lila saw a card behind Kima's chair. It must have fallen when Kima pulled out the paper.

When Miss Janet returned to the front of the room, Lila brought her pencil to the sharpener near Kima's desk. The card had a heart on one side and '*You're such a beauty*' written on the other.

No wonder Kima was smiling, Lila thought to herself. She glanced around the room. Had anyone else seen it? She didn't think so. Did Kima know who had sent it?

Pencil sharpened, she headed back to her desk, stooping to pick up the card on her way. She placed it on Kima's desk with a whisper. "I think you dropped this."

That Friday was Lila's birthday. Her mother baked a big cake for her to bring to school. During the lunch break, her class sang her Happy Birthday and gave Lila homemade cards.

Lila read them while everyone ate the cake. She was surprised to see one from Kima. She smiled as she opened it, only to be shocked by the message. *We are here for the cake. Nobody cares about your birthday.*

Looking up, her eyes met Kima's smirk. Lila straightened and smiled. "Thank you very much."

Lila quickly placed the card at the bottom of the pile so no one else would see it. She was hurt, but didn't tell Laura. Laura already disliked Kima and if she learned of this, she would tell miss Janet, who would tell Mama. Lila had come to this school to get a fresh start, she didn't want to be the bullied kid again. At the end of the day, Lila brought home all of her cards to show her mother. Except for Kima's. That she left in her locker. When the school day was over, she had stayed a little longer in the classroom trying to decide what to do with the card.

Before putting it in her locker, she had seen something interesting on the class calendar. She was hatching a plan.

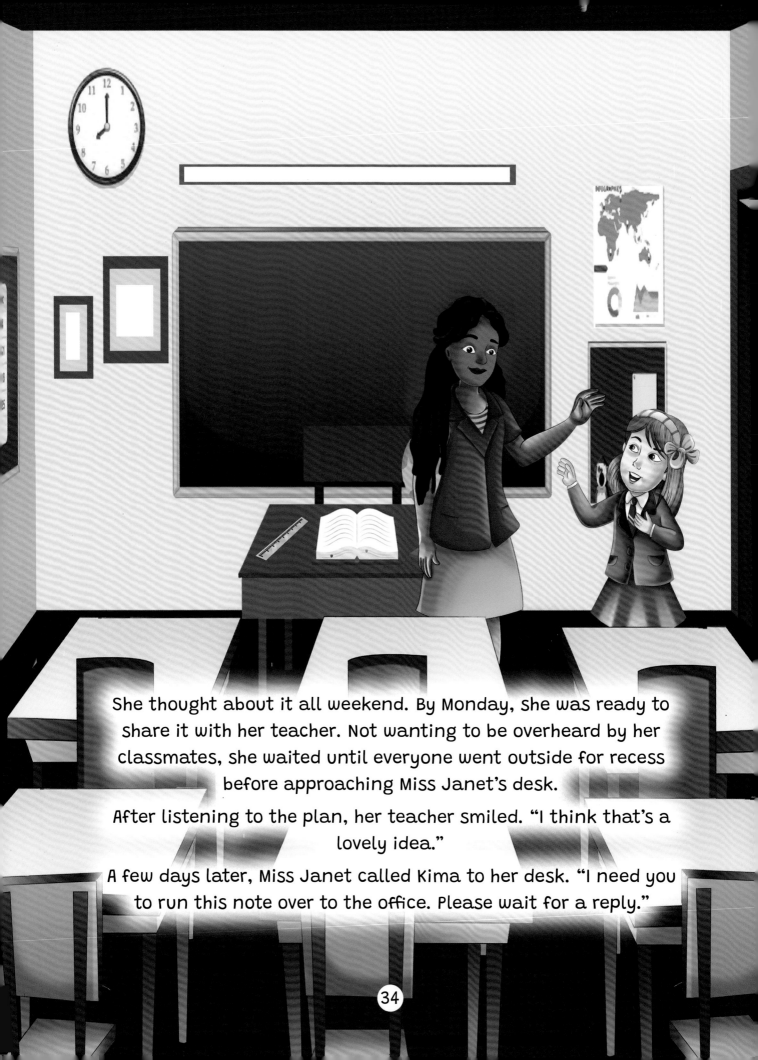

She thought about it all weekend. By Monday, she was ready to share it with her teacher. Not wanting to be overheard by her classmates, she waited until everyone went outside for recess before approaching Miss Janet's desk.

After listening to the plan, her teacher smiled. "I think that's a lovely idea."

A few days later, Miss Janet called Kima to her desk. "I need you to run this note over to the office. Please wait for a reply."

As soon as Kima left the room, Miss Janet nodded to Lila. Standing at her desk, Lila glanced at her class. "I need your help with something," she told them.

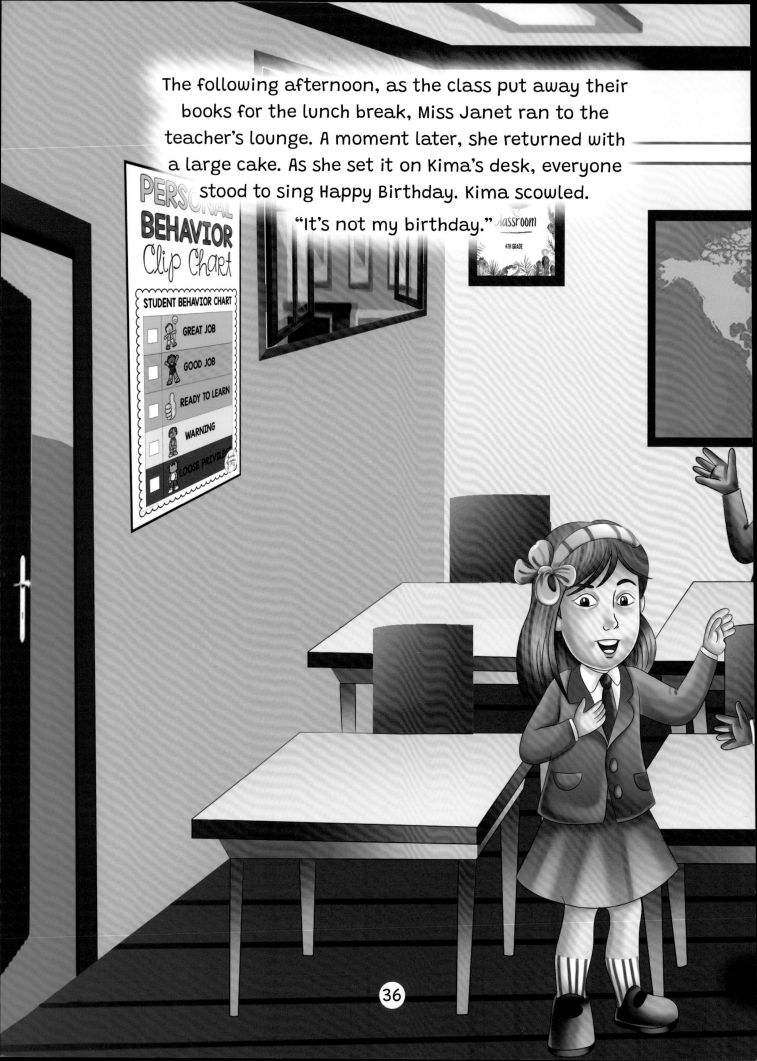

The following afternoon, as the class put away their books for the lunch break, Miss Janet ran to the teacher's lounge. A moment later, she returned with a large cake. As she set it on Kima's desk, everyone stood to sing Happy Birthday. Kima scowled.

"It's not my birthday."

PERSONAL
BEHAVIOR
Clip Chart

STUDENT BEHAVIOR CHART

GREAT JOB

GOOD JOB

READY TO LEARN

WARNING

LOOSE PRIVILEGES

Classroom

4TH GRADE

Miss Janet smiled. "I'm sorry we missed it last week. Lila saw the date on the calendar and planned this."

The students piled their cards on Kima's desk before hurrying to the front of the room where Miss Janet was serving cake.

Lila stayed behind, handing Kima the card she had made. "Happy Belated Birthday."

Kima eyed her warily. Grabbing the card, she read it silently. Lila saw the shock on Kima's face. Without a word, Kima rummaged through her desk, pulling out the card from her secret admirer. She glared at Lila.

"You? You put this card in my locker last week?"

Lila nodded. "I want to be your friend."

Kima shoved both cards in her desk. "I don't need friends. Get lost."

Disappointed, Lila went to get her cake. As she reached the front of the room, she glanced over her shoulder. Kima was smiling at the two cards Lila had given her.

When Lila went to use the bathroom at the end of the day, she heard someone crying as soon as she walked in. All the stalls were empty. Around the corner, she found Kima sitting on the floor.

"Are you okay?"

"Go away!"

Lila joined Kima on the floor, she had been so confident before but now Lila was wondering whether this had been a bad idea and she had made things worse.

"What's wrong? Didn't you like your surprise?"

Kima sniffed. "No one's ever given me a birthday party before."

Lila's eyes went wide. "Really?"

"My mom? She's never around. She works three jobs to support me and my little brother and sometimes she forgets things like my birthday."

Lila got to her feet. "Come on."

Kima gave her a confused look. "Where?"

"You're coming to my house. We'll play pin the tail on the donkey and have a birthday party. Maybe my mom will even make another cake."

Kima stood with a sniffle. "Your mom made me that cake? Why?"

"I wanted you to have a happy birthday."

To Lila's surprise, Kima threw her arms around her, squeezing her tight. "Thank you! For my cake, for putting that card in my locker. Thank you."

Lila beamed, her plan had worked and now she had made a new friend. "Come on. We have a party to make."

When Kima's mother came to retrieve her after supper, she joined Lila's mother for a cup of coffee in the kitchen. "I'm so glad Kima's found a friend."

Kima scoffed as she entered the kitchen. "My friend threw me a birthday party."

Lila could see the pain in Kima's mother's face. "Oh, baby. Did I forget again?"

When Kima nodded, tears formed in her mother's eyes. "I'm so sorry. It's not that I don't know when your birthday is. I just have no idea what day it is anymore. I remember the day you were born like it was yesterday. It was one of the happiest days of my life."

43

Kima crossed her arms. "I know you're busy… but you don't check on us or bother to write down our birthdays. I just… I didn't know if you still cared about me." Although Kima looked tough, her voice was starting to break and tears were lining her eyes.

Her mother pulled her into a hug. "Baby, everything I do is because I love you. I want to be the best mom in the whole wide world. You tell me how."

Kima gave her mother a skeptical look. "You mean it?"

When her mother nodded, she uncrossed her arms and hugged her mother tightly. "I just wanted to know that, for sure. Thank you mom."

That night, Lila's mother knocked on her bedroom door. "I'm very proud of you."

"For what?"

"You won over that bully with love."

Lila looked at her mother, surprise marking her face. "Why did you call her a bully?"

Her mother sat beside her on the bed. "I heard her apologize to you earlier. Now it's my turn to apologize."

"For what?"

"When you were being bullied at Summerhill, you wanted me to talk to Mr. Clarke. But, I wouldn't."

Lila shrugged. "That's okay."

"No, it's not. Sweetie, the reason I didn't want to talk to Mr. Clarke was because I was embarrassed. When we were in fifth grade, I was very mean to Mr. Clarke. Frankly, I was afraid of going to Summerhill, knowing I might run into him. I was ashamed of how I treated him. But you've taught Mama something priceless."

"I have?"

Her mother nodded. "You've taught me that some bullies can be won over with love. Thanks for asking me to bake that cake."

"Thanks for reading. If you enjoyed the story, please consider leaving a review where you bought it."

Author Bio

Ife Akanegbu has always had a lifelong passion for telling stories. Upon observing the alarming rise in depression, anxiety, and self-harm rates, he felt compelled to take action and he knew his gift for storytelling could make a difference. That's when he combined this talent with his more than fifteen years of medical expertise to create Motivating Our Champions, a game-changing children's book series designed to help our precious little ones take good care of their mental health.

Ife's charming life story is full of inspiration, adventure, and compassion. In fact, he has mastered the art of captivating storytelling by sharing his thrilling experiences with others. Ultimately, this motivated him to use his skill to impact current mental health trends, an issue that concerns him deeply. The practitioner completed his medical training in Nigeria before achieving a Master's in Health Management at the University of Leeds. He now practices family medicine in British Columbia, where he lives with his wife and daughter.

Ife Akanegbu